G000066564

Gold Adornments and
other stories

Gold Adornments and other stories

EMMA KITTLE-PEY

Patrician Press ● Manningtree

First published as a paperback edition by Patrician Press 2017

E-book edition published by Patrician Press 2017

www.patricianpress.com

Copyright © Emma Kittle-Pey 2017

The right of Emma Kittle-Pey to be identified as the author of this work has been asserted in accordance with the Copyright, Designs and Patents Act of 1988.

All rights reserved. No part of this document may be reproduced or transmitted in any form or by any means, electronic, mechanical, photocopying, recording, or otherwise, without prior written permission of Patrician Press.

British Library Cataloguing in Publication Data. A catalogue record for this book is available from the British Library.

ISBN paperback edition 978-0-9955386-9-6

ISBN e-book edition 978-0-9955386-8-9

www.patricianpress.com

Contents

Published by Patrician Press 2017
For more information: www.patricianpress.com

Napoleon ended his speech with a reminder of Boxer's two favourite maxims, 'I will work harder' and 'Comrade Napoleon is always right' – maxims, he said, which every animal would do well to adopt as his own.

George Orwell, *Animal Farm*

For Harvey and Esme
All the ways

In these short and often witty vignettes and stories, Emma Kittle-Pey delves below the surface of the everyday, exposing the extraordinary way we deal with the reality of home, work and human interaction. Through her unique observation, Emma reflects on the ways in which ordinary people adapt and deal with the fundamental changes taking place in the wider political and economic climate, and survive.

This is Emma's second short story collection for Patrician Press. Her first was *Fat Maggie and other stories* published in 2013 and reprinted in 2017.

Emma is studying for a PhD in Creative Writing at the University of Essex. She is host of Colchester community writing group, WriteNight. Website: ekpey.com Twitter: @ekittl, @colwritenight

'Emma Kittle-Pey has a way of scratching beneath the surface of everyday interaction. She picks out the key details of ordinary events which reveal new meanings.'

Sarah Armstrong

The charity shop

wars

I'd made the journey all the way from London to the estuary town of Collingtree, but after eventually finding parking on one of the steep narrow roads leading from the high street, I knock at my Aunt Jean's bungalow door to find she isn't in. No sign of the dogs either. I have to admit I'm a bit disappointed. On the way here I had the good idea that she might try help out her favourite nephew with a bit of cash, just to tide me over of course, like she used to.

I think I'll hang around just for a bit to see if she'll come back, she might just be walking the dogs or something. But the grey sky I followed here finally cracks and I duck into what I thought was a hardware store. Turns out it's a Pet Rescue charity shop, a kind of pop up charity shop. The two ladies at the counter stare at me for a moment before one of them turns her attention back to a girl looking through some junk.

'Are you slim under there, love? Skinny? *Gorgeous* slip over here. *Sexy.* Suit a lovely young thing like you.' The object of their attention is a girl in a purple hat and a large overcoat, who turns and flares her nostrils at me.

'What is it you're after, love?' One of the ladies is right next to her, and I begin to pretend to look through the books.

'A round knitting needle,' she says.

'Oh where have I seen one? I know I've seen one somewhere. *I* know. I have one at home,' says the shop assistant. 'Are you local?'

'I work at the health food store, I've just started,' says the girl in the hat.

'I'll get it for you, bring it, bring it to the shop if you like. I'll do it tomorrow.'

'That's very kind of you,' says the girl. I have a peek over and I see her delicate pink cheek.

'Yes, I'll find it tonight and bring it to you tomorrow. What was your name?'

'Sarah.'

'I'll do that for you then, Sarah.' The woman goes back to her place behind the glass counter and the two ladies serving at the Pet Rescue charity shop counter continue to chat.

I start to wander around. The place is a mess, and full of junk. Cheap creased shoes and small ceramic earthenware from the mid-90s. I can smell that gurchy musty smell and a waft of something acrid rising from the warming damp of my coat.

The first voice is loud again. 'That pompous Miranda,' she says. 'Always feel like she's looking down on me, know what I mean, Brenda?'

'That's what she's like isn't it.'

'Don't know how she got like that, do you?'

'Don't know how any of us get the way we are. We just do, don't we?'

The rain on the crowded window is cocooning us in, a water

curtain steaming up at the edges. It's warm in here. Maybe too warm. I stop in front of a gold cabinet and look at a basket of odds and ends, listening to the women, aware of the girl. I let out a little laugh when I pick up a round stone and wonder if she notices. But then, on the flat side, underneath, I see that it is not just a stone but a fossil. I hold it within my palm carefully so it cannot be seen by them and look at the imprint. It's an imprint of a fish. A fish with feet.

Now I know, that in the shop I pass everyday on the Kensington Church Street, the one on my way back from work, that beautiful fossils go for an arm and a leg. I walk home slowly, looking in the windows, dragging the time before I get back. And now I feel a small tremor bubble in my belly.

'What you got, love?' Brenda is standing right beside me.

'I was just thinking that my son would love this to add to his collection of stones.'

'Ooh, yes, I'm sure,' she says. 'Haven't you got a game about telling the time behind there Jill? She's got a game about telling the time behind there, I bet he would like that too.'

'Yes, I'm sure,' I say. Jill sighs and drops down from her stool.

'It'll be a great game for learning to tell the time,' she says, 'the little boy will love it. What's his name?'

'Um. Sebastian.'

'Here it is.' Jill lifts a plastic board game onto the counter. Some of the numbers are missing. 'I think they're in the box. That's a lovely one for your kid.'

'Yes, I'm sure he would love it. So how much is it?'

'£1?'

'And for the rock?' '

'£1.50 altogether.' I search through my pockets and can't find anything now. Not even a penny. Nothing in my wallet either.

'Can you hold them for me while I go and get some cash? 'As

long as you come back,' Jill says. 'I mean the clock game won't hang around forever. I bet someone would love that clock game. You got any kids, love?'

'No,' says the purple-hatted girl, still looking at the knitting needles.

'Don't you worry,' I say, 'I'm an honest man, I'll be back in a jiff,' flashing them a wide grin. The bell rattles as I open the door and run through the rain to the cash point over the road. Rushing to type my pin I get it wrong. I hear the bell tinkle, and I flick my eyes towards the shop door which is just closing. The cash point is beeping at me. Do I want a receipt yes or no? YES I mean, NO.

'*Here's* the honest gentleman,' Brenda sighs. 'Your purchases are all wrapped up for you sir.'

Jill hands over a creased and yellowed Morrison's bag with the plastic clock game and a package wrapped in newspaper inside. 'We don't have no change for a tenner. Don't get many customers buying things with notes in here,' she shouts.

They both look at me and I say, 'Well, you'd better keep the change, ladies.'

'Are you sure? That's VERY kind of you. That's very kind isn't it, Jill? He's honest AND kind.'

'Don't get many like that, do you?' Jill booms as I hold the bag away from my coat cuff.

'Not at all. And can I just say that you ladies are doing a great job here, at the...' I search for an indication of the charity's name '... Pet Rescue.'

Holding my prize carefully and yet consciously I wonder what other treasures I might find I this small town. Wonder what it's worth? Even within my view are two other charity shops on this very same street.

The second charity shop is a pile of crap too. But I'm careful to scan the place, the worn clothes, the kids' stuff for a pound, the bric-a-brac.

I cross the road and am thinking about getting back to Jean's now when I see the other one, which looks more like a ladies clothes shop, but as I look closely I can see a few royal wedding mugs. It's another charity shop – Melth. As I enter, they're hoovering. 'Oh pardon me,' I say, 'are you closing?'

'Ooh no,' says the bobbed elderly lady, 'just trying to fit it in between customers!'

'Ah good.' I wander around, appreciating the spacious, well managed racks of clothes. A nice zigzagged scarf in the men's section I see is £15. £15. And it looks worn around the edges. But still, the shop's more pleasant to peruse: bigger, airier, spacious and neat. In the bric-a-brac section one of the ladies is on her knees, moving things around. I hear her sniff gently before she moves out of my way. I hear her whisper, 'That's all done Miranda.' I scan the shelves above where she was dusting. On a little wire stand, could have been made especially for it, is a fossil just like the one I have in the bag.

As I stare at it I feel none of the earlier excitement. What a fool, I say to myself. A tenner for that old stone. When really they're ten a penny. What a goddam fool. Jean never knew that about me, did she? Can't get anything right. So I leave the shop, still conscious of the dirty wrinkled carrier bag in my hand.

The sky is darkening as I head back toward the street where the car is parked. The rain's stopped but I'm shivering. Forget Jean and her dogs. I get in and fling the bag onto the seat. As I pass the estuary the swans are still strutting about. I push down the window and cast it out towards them, hoping I might hit one. I put down my foot and get the hell out of there.

As I work at my desk, getting the figures to balance for the taxman, I turn to see the close up of the fossil on the muted TV screen. I grab the controller and switch on the sound. The stone fish darts away and there is a local news reporter talking to a young girl with pink cheeks. 'So you say you found it here? In a charity shop?'

'Yes, at the Melth shop. Over there. I showed it to my boss and he said that he knew of a pair of fish fossils a local woman had once owned that were said to be really important, but she hid them away and no-one ever knew if the story was true. So it made me wonder if *this* could be, and I took it to an old chap at Fulton. Knows everything about the teeth and remains found around here.' The news cuts amateurishly, in my view, to a red tower and a windy cliff.

'And here he is,' says the newscaster, hair flipping over her eyes. A man with a white beard and an army hat stands bewildered, staring at the camera.

'So what can you tell us about the Collingtree fish fossils?' she asks.

'I been doing this job for fifty years and I discovered 53 million year old sharks' teeth but I never seen anything as ancient as this. It's the walking fish. Probably 375 million years old! For hundreds of years people have told the story of the east coast walking fish. A local myth. And here's the evidence to back up the stories.'

'And are you aware of the value of these stones to evolutionary scientists?'

Pause. 'I just said, didn't I ?'

Pause. 'And you mentioned that from your knowledge of fish-life you would say that this was a male specimen?'

'Yes. We're thrilled about this. Look carefully at the pockets around the bottom here we think you can see the male reproductive organ, known as the clasper.'

'I see it there yes.' Pause. 'But, more to the point, what does it mean for the mental health charity, Melth? And the value of this fossil?'

'Well... the fossil's priceless,' he smiles. 'The only thing *more* valuable to us would be having a fossil of the female fish, given that we'd then have a pair. As far as a monetary value is concerned let's just say, the charity and the girl who's sharing it with them are very lucky.'

'And there you have it. A giant story in a small town, a very kind young girl, and a lot of money for the mental health charity, Melth. I don't think you could have a better story than that, but I wonder if Bill can beat it with his weather news?'

I think back to the moment when I opened the car window, the yellow bag and the waft of stale cigarette disappearing after it as I flung it out towards the river. My heart has sunk into my stomach but a little bit of my brain says, it might still be there. There's something else though. I'm not sure what it is. A flickering image of Brenda and the smelly Pet Rescue charity shop. There's something uncomfortable happening. My heart's flickering along with the images – Jean and her dirty windows, Brenda and the Pet Rescue shop. An honest gentleman. Maybe they could do with a bit of luck too.

I like your necklace

In Willie Gees Kate bought a bra. The young girl at the counter said, *I like your necklace.*

Kate thought, *even though you are probably doing that thing where you're supposed to pick out something personal to make the shopping experience more intimate, to make me feel special, to make me come back, I am going to go along with the compliment anyway, and tell the story of where it came from and how I remember them having a little table at a market stall on Brick Lane and how now there's a shop behind Neal Street, and they even sell their stuff on ASOS.*

And while she was saying it, Kate at least was enjoying her own story, a little slice of her history that she was remodelling. The counter girl might of course be interested in how a young lady who was that way inclined, could make a go of it with something creative, and it might get her somewhere, rather than standing behind this counter paying fake compliments. Or she might not have been expecting that amount of detail about the necklace as a response to saying she liked it, in which case it was also quite enjoyable to watch her, as Kate enthused about the necklace, the story, the history, thinking she was asking a genuine question rather than a pretend one. Anyway, the girl had a big smile on her face because, either way, it appeared the compliment had worked.

Kate felt quite a bit happier after that fake conversation, maybe as opposed to no conversation at all. She thought, that night, she'd go back again and get the matching knickers.

It was the following Saturday in the end, luckily the knickers were still there in the sale. Kate took them to the counter and the same girl was there wearing a necklace just like hers. Kate said, *I like your necklace*, with a knowing smile, and the shop girl said, *thanks, it's from ASOS – they started out with a market stall on Brick Lane, now they have a shop behind Neal Street. Cool eh?* Kate frowned a little as the girl tapped the buttons on the till and packed the knickers into a small bag. She felt her hair, fuzzier today than before maybe. Kate waited for her to say something else but she didn't, the girl in the necklace handed her the bag and said, *great knickers, love the colour.*

The fat of the land

We saw Madman had made another dump of his weird rubbish at the very far corner of the farmer's field again. Michael couldn't resist picking up a stick and running towards it, trampling the hard stems of the chopped wheat as he ran. How I wanted his trainers right then. I glanced at the windows of the Madhouse, alone on the edge of the new housing estate, sitting between us and the farm to the east. Its black windows and stillness made me shudder.

By the time I caught up, Michael was bashing the side of the pile, beating up a white ash storm. I stood on the edge, careful of my new shoes, staring at the carcass of a book; singed pages lifting, floating and fluttering around us in flakes. He picked up the strap of a grey lace bra with his stick and flicked it onto the peak. 'Wonder whose that was?' I looked toward the house, a shadow moved in an upstairs window.

It was then I saw the glimpses of orange, eyeing us from inside, from the core of the mound. I stepped back, noticing my shoes were covered with a fine white coat. Underneath they were beginning to melt, a thin plastic tide was retreating from the heat before I did.

I moved away fast to protect them. I shouted to him, 'Stop–Look, Michael!'

But he didn't listen, or if he did he couldn't resist another couple of whacks, each more powerful than the last. The ash clouds bellowed up into the clay-blue sky, a flash of sun as the window creaked, and when I looked back at him Michael was rolling around the ground on his back, holding his left cheek where the dump had spat and hit him in the face.

I forgot my shoes, and ran as fast as I could to the gate of the house. But the door was already opening and I stopped to see the man we'd whispered about for so long, his big hair and bushy beard, his small bare chest and green army trousers, pulling out a bucket of water and a packet of lard.

A little piece of England

When he had looked out of his window yesterday morning, he had seen it obscuring the view of the road. Who could have done it? Why was it there? He found his phone and tapped in the number on the front of the sign. It went onto answer machine.

As he poured the treacly tea from the pot he was still thinking about it. Had his kids put his house up for sale? Had his eldest phoned the estate agent and told them he wanted to move? That was probably it. He took his phone and tapped *Recents*, Mark was always first on the list of the latest calls. He heard his son scuffling with phone before putting it to his ear.

'What is it Dad? It's early.'

'Did you phone the estate agents? And tell them I wanted the house on the market?'

'No.' Pause. 'But I did say something to Jess.'

'What do you mean?'

'I said I thought it might be a good idea. I didn't think she'd do anything about it.'

13

For the first time, Jack hung up on his eldest son.

Heart pumping now, he called the number on the sign again.

'Eazymove. How can I help?'

'I have a sign in my garden that I have not asked for and I would like someone to come and remove it.'

'We don't usually put signs in gardens that aren't asked for.'

He can almost hear her hairspray. 'Well, you have. I'd like you to come and take it away. Right now.'

'The sign fitters are not working today but I'll see if they can see you tomorrow. What's the address?'

'83 Thornton Road.'

'I'll make a note and someone will call you back later.'

'Oh very professional,' he rasps as he put the phone down again. Next he taps in Jess's number.

'Hi Dad,' she says. He can hear his grandson squealing in the background.

'Did you ask the estate agents to put the house on the market?'

'Whose house?'

'Mine.'

'Here Alfie.' Her voice becomes distant. 'It's Grandad. No, you don't have to speak to him. Yours? Why would I put yours on the market?'

'Mark said he talked to you about it.'

'Did he? He might have done.'

'Well, did you phone the estate agents or not?' he shouts.

'No. It's not for your nose, Alfie. Jen said you might get on better somewhere more modern, less work to do. It might have been her.'

'Jesus Christ!' And he hangs up on his second child for the first time.

All day he sees the sign. When he goes to his shift at the fish factory he has to walk past it and when he comes home he spots it from the end of the road. He tries to push it down. It falls easily on the second push and he leaves the sign down on the grass at the front of the house.

Least it's out of view. But he still feels anger at the estate agent for not coming to remove their sign, for his daughter for going behind his back. It was probably all of them. Trying to do what's best. Trying to take over. Trying to make out he needs help all of a sudden.

The next day he tries again. The minute they open. 'Is someone coming to collect my sign?'

'Which sign?' Says the woman on the other end of the line.

'83 Thornton Road,' he says. 'I have a sign and I would like someone to remove it because I never asked for the sign and I want someone to come and take it away.'

'83 Thornton, you say? I don't have a record of 83 Thornton Road.'

'I'm telling you that there is a sign in my garden and I want someone to come and take it away. Today.'

'Okay sir.' Sigh. 'I'll speak to the sign team and see what they can do.'

'Thank you!' Seething now, he puts the phone down again.

Next he calls Jen. Before he speaks she says, 'The answer's no.'

'What do you mean?'

'It wasn't me.' And she puts the phone down before he does.

He stares at the sign. He spends the morning looking out of the window at the sign lying on the grass. The sign people do not come. He thinks about how things have changed, about how the children are trying to be the grown-ups now. Like they have some idea that that's supposed to happen, something they've heard. Like he's an old man.

The time for him to go to work is getting nearer. The sign is making his blood boil.

He goes to his shed and gets out a saw and his bench and measures the post into six inch parts. Each break takes him a while. He keeps sawing the sign until he has a pile of parts. He puts them in his shopping bag and before it is time to go to work he walks the bag into the town centre where he finds the glossy window of the estate agents and pushes open the door. She doesn't even look up to greet him before he gets to her desk. He lifts the bag up high and upturns it so that the wood blocks fall like giant pellets, and the sawdust blows up into the air, a dirty cloud filling their sanitised workspace. Then for a bit of a finale he slams the plastic Eazymove sign down on the top.

'38 Thornton,' she cries. 'It was supposed to be for no 38. Not 83. We worked out the problem. We meant to call you. The sign guys were coming over this afternoon!' The rest of the agents in the room are standing up with their hands in the air, as though he's some kind of terrorist.

'Too bloody late.'

He walks out of there, heart still throbbing and gets to work seven minutes earlier than usual.

Gold adornments

I took an apple from the yellow bowl and sketched it in pencil. Filling it with paint, thickening the layers, balancing the colours on the canvas, I painted in the red shiny skin and the lopsided stalk.

That evening, when I went to visit, my mother said, 'We're going to stop at the station soon. Don't want too many other passengers on here.'

'Mum,' I put my hand on hers, 'We're not on a train now, we're at the new home.'

Ida came with some tea, and to see how we were getting on. 'How's the journey, Mrs Smith?'

'Fine, thank you. But where's Jim?'

'Mum,' I nipped in before Ida could lie, 'Dad died. Don't you remember?'

'Dead? No. He was here a moment ago.' Sunshine wobbled in her small hooded eyes. 'Dead? I was wondering where he was.'

Every day I sketched and painted that apple. I watched as it softened and wrinkled and the colour jaded. It took longer than I expected. When I was painting the sixteenth, my grandson came to visit me. He pulled a wooden train along the lines of the room.

That evening I took him with me to see his great grandma. She smiled as the little boy pushed the train the length of the bed-rail.

The next day, I opened the patio doors. Taking my easel into the garden, I set it up by the tree, and drew, my skull caressed by a fruity symphony of birdsong, my chest rattling as the trains rumbled by. A charcoal mist filled my nose and settled like chalk-dust at the back of my throat. I followed the white haze down to the station and sketched the celebrated steam train. Filling it with paint, thickening the layers, and balancing the colours on the canvas, I painted in the green shiny coat and the gold adornments.

The train picture went in a frame, and on the hook by my mother's bed. A beam lifted her face, opened her eyes. 'That's right. Just there, by the engine. Jim will like that. Where is he?'

'He's just nipped to the loo, Mum,' I said. My grandson pulled his train around the edge of the rug, and over to the corner with the chair, where Ida was sitting reading Woman's Own in the new 'waiting room'.

The animal team

Ida called the council, before they opened, the moment they opened. She didn't think he could hear the urgency in her voice. He put her on hold.

'Someone could come out Wednesday,' he said after seventeen minutes.

'That's two days! Of scratching, scurrying claws,' Ida said. 'Of being scared to go in the kitchen!'

But Wednesday it was, and they came in their van. The Animal Team. One beamed over a rotund belly and under a shiny bald head; the other, leaning over him, yellow-skinned and wrinkled, remained poker faced. She took them into her kitchen, showed them her traps, the blue poison she left in the place the pests had discovered her potatoes.

'Not much we can do,' he said, 'we'll put down more poison, but looks like you've already done the right thing,' tapping one of the plastic traps she'd put down with the side of his trainer, noticing the wedge of black hair caught in the lock. 'Must be bigguns,' he laughed. 'To get away from that.'

'Where did they come from?' Ida asked.

'We've had a look but as all the houses are link attached they could be coming in anywhere.'

'Can you look under the cupboards? Can you find out?'

'No. We don't have the tools.'

'How can I find out where they're coming in? I thought that's what I was paying you for.'

'We put down the poison and we can't see where they're coming in,' the round one was still smirking at her, the other turning his body to go. 'Can't do much more than that. Should be fine now anyway, looks like they took some of the poison. It'll just take them a few days to cop it.'

They climbed back in their Animal Team van. The older man sat back and rolled a cigarette. 'Nice one,' he said. 'You're learning. Fill in that form.' He stuffed the paperwork onto his new partner's lap.

'Where's the next job then?'

'Hold your horses,' he said, flicking up the yellow strand falling from a slick of white greasy hair. 'We've got plenty of time. Supposed to be an hour or more per visit, if you count searching and blocking entries etc. That's what we're doing now right?' He raised an eyebrow at his colleague.

As they set off, the old man said, 'Stop.' He got out of the car and emptied his bag of food scraps, sticky bacon rind and veg from his dinner last night, into one of the broken drain covers at the end of the road. 'Got to keep us in work right?' he says as he climbs back in. 'Got to feed the family right?' His new friend's smile tightened.

'Right Gov. Where next?'

That night Ida was down on her knees, bum in the air, cheek to the floor, with a torch and a hammer, just in case. She retched over and over at the thought of a black monster springing into her face. She took away the kickboard under the sink, chest and hammer braced for a rat to spring out, but there were none, just some half eaten blue bags of poison. She couldn't see a way in, just as the men had said.

She could still hear the scratches and the snuffles in the night. Her dreams and waking moments merged into each other and her night was full of rats and flees and rabies and monsters and seething and wheels of thoughts. She called the council the next morning, before she could, the moment she could.

'I can still hear them!'

'We can come again, but it actually takes the rats three or four days to die anyway.'

The girl spoke as though Ida was worrying about the weather. It was no use. She wrenched out more of the kickboards and found an awkward hole, broken chipped concrete around the edge of a water pipe. She looked up what to do on the Kindle Fire her daughter had got her for Christmas.

She filled the hole with steel wire and cement.

After that, Ida didn't see any more signs in the kitchen, and especially when she knew it was dry, she began to relax. But if she slept lightly, or had another night of circling thoughts, she could hear scuffling in the distance and she imagined a maze through the link attached houses and the rats coming up her pipe and bashing their noses on her concrete job.

Last of the day

He's put on the plastic glasses and is pulling open her top lip. A little jab, and a sharp bitter taste runs along the top of her gum. This must be an anaesthetic, Ida thinks. He didn't mention that, did he?

'Which tooth?' He had said earlier, testing, jesting with her.

'Don't you know?' She asked back, quick but true.

'Top or bottom?'

'Top.' She remembers that much at least.

'Number 3 or number 6?'

'3?'

'No, 6!'

Handsome fellow, smile winking at her. 'I like my patients to know what I'm doing. I know a story about a doctor who went to take out a kidney and took out the healthy one!' The tennis is on a screen above her head. Henman is there. She tries to read the subtitles but her eyelids are drooping. A shot of David Beckham and sons in the crowd.

'Open wide,' he says. She wrenches open her eyes and her dodgy old jaw clicks as she stretches it further. She realizes she doesn't even worry about it any more.

The two of them, the dentist and the nurse, are there in front of her now, taking turns to insert their tools into her mouth. 'Open wide!' he says again. She yanks her aching clicking jaw open wider. Prodding, scratching, cracking.

'Not much longer,' he says as he puts something around the tooth, a rubber coated clamp. 'You can relax your jaw.' The two of them are close now, Ida can smell his rubber fingers there. She relaxes her jaw and the words on the screen are too much for her. She closes her eyes. She is inside her mouth.

Prodding. Poking. She knows exactly where it is now. Top right. Is that a 'careful' the nurse says quietly? Maybe not. 'Light!' he shouts. 'Look!' he says. More prodding. She can smell something acrid, is it the rubber or his breath? He's saying 'bite' now and she is inside her mouth biting something flat between her teeth. 'How does it feel?'

'Okay?' What if it's not okay, what if she can't tell and she says it's okay and it's not okay?

'Is it flush?'

What does flush mean? Does it mean flat? She doesn't know if it's flat. She's not sure.

She can feel him sanding her tooth vigorously, a long white gravelly cement trough sanded by a giant metal nail file, back and forth, back and forth, quick like he knows what he's doing. Or he's rushing. There he is again, sanding it down. And now done.

She opens her eyes, she is outside her mouth. He stands in front of her, peeling off his gloves. Was that a little look he gave his nurse? Was that a little bowing of her head and a whisking away to get on with something else? Ida can't be sure what that was.

She gets up off the chair and straightens herself out and by the time she's ready he's back, looking at his screen. He swivels his chair and smiles. 'The reason I said bring me the light', he says smirking, 'is that I saw a crack, a big crack under the filling, that's why the other one didn't work and you needed a new one. Usually I have to have a magnifying glass to see the crack, but with yours I can just see it with the light. Anyway I've filled it again but underneath is a crack, and let's just see if this filling works and if not we know why.'

Ida's just staring at him going 'oh okay', thinking this must be the modern way, to know everything, just like he said, to know which of your own teeth need filling, which number they are, to know that something is going on under that painless tooth that could soon mean something, the start of something truly horrendous, the likes of which she's never experienced, the pain of an infected tooth, the removal of a tooth? The first step towards missing teeth, not her own teeth, old age? Death even?

He smiles and says, 'that's it then,' swinging his chair away. It's the end of their day, he's said it; the nurse doesn't look around. Ida was last of the day.

Milanese feast

As the murmur of voices buzzed around my head I began to hear just hear one soloist, coming from behind where I sat at the breakfast table.

'We're in Milan. People go shopping in Milan. It's like Manhattan. If we're not going shopping then I might as well go. Are you going to give me some money? Are you *not* going to give me some money?'

I sought her out in the reflections of the window. I could see a teenager with her parents. Staring at her phone. A primadonna. I went back to my pile of carbs from the all-you-can-eat buffet. I got everything, there was still an abundance of food even when I arrived. I'd been expecting it ravaged and savaged, but no; an overflowing tray of croissants, and pastries, a bucket of cake, biscuits in a bottomless pot. Fruit, half peaches, yoghurt, cereals. Ham, cheese, apricots. I tried not to overdo it, but it was hard.

'It's Milan. You've got to give me money. Oh god. You're not going to. That really sucks.'

I ate my croissants, and drank my juice. I stared out of the window. It wasn't what I'd expected from Milan, the view of a concrete terrace I'd have found at home. But it didn't matter. To be alone, for no one to know, to stop the constant living of two lives, the one inside and the one for show. To stop everything.

The men beside me chatted, I could see the intensity in the face of the guy from earlier. He'd pranced to one of the spare tables and put his bag on a seat, claiming it as his own, moaning and whining to his partner about the queue. But their voices were dull in comparison to the girl behind me. The ache above my eyes was prodded by her notes, her tune in crescendo.

'You want me to take my tray over there?'

'I want you to take your tray over there.' Her dad a resolute double bass to her vivace violin.

'I'm not taking my tray over there. It's full up.'

'I want you to take your tray over there. Because that's what people do.'

Her voice swayed above the swarm of voices, soaring over it now like an angry clarinet. But the buzz settled, reduced, quietened for her performance. The men next to me, and other heads, started to look around a little too.

'I'm not taking the tray. I can see some other people not taking their trays.'

'I want you to give me your cell-phone and take the tray.'

I turned again, properly, toward this voice.

I saw the girl looking at the tray area and back again and to it again. 'Are you trying to humiliate me?' She says.

'No. Give me your cell phone and take the tray.'

It was that tiny uncomfortable fidgeting look she gave the tray trolley. And then the second one. And the third.

The ache left my head, fell into the back of my throat and sank into my stomach. I remembered a hundred moments of our youth in that second and I nearly wept for her and him, and the mum that had already left them to it.

I got up with my tray and as I passed I stopped at their table. 'I'm taking my tray. Do you want to come with me?'

The girl stared at my navel, the dad looked up and said, 'We don't speak.'

But I did it again. I thrust my idea forward, I risked everything, and I said, 'But do you want to just come with me? I'm taking my tray.'

The girl rose, head bent, with her tray, and the dad said, 'Oh. Thank you.' She followed me to the tray trolley. There was no room. We lifted them onto the top, the glass of orange juice sliding to one side above my head, but I somehow managed to balance it before it fell. First my tray, then hers.

Goodbye to Mary
and all that

Bob hears the pip of the ambulance before he sees its flashing blue lights, and stepping up in the name of new-found-community-spirit, he puts his hand out to stop the car approaching, which tries to swerve around but brakes just a shriek from his feet.

On the other side of the road cars are lining the pavement, and have left enough room for the ambulance to spin through. Once it's gone he pulls his lollipop stick away, out of the road, and the red face of the woman in the car passes him by.

The cars stream back into order and he waits to see if anyone else wants to cross this morning. No one comes and he makes his way back, to the convenience shop, where he looks at the Indian vegetables; he picks out one he hasn't used yet and takes it to the counter. 'What do I do with this?' He asks the lady standing there.

'Well,' she smiles, for this is not the first time this week. She holds up the marrow and mimes peeling it and then dicing as she explains, and then she says 'wait,' she brings him some beans, a few potatoes, an onion, some curry powder and coconut milk.

'Here, chop all of these put them in a pot and cook for forty minutes.'

'How much?'

'No you take it, see if you like the *lauki*, if you do you can get some more.' As she speaks she's packing it neatly into a wafer thin bag.

So at home he does as she had said. The kitchen is clean, ready for his task. 'Not so hard,' he thinks as he makes a neat pile of the vegetable on the chopping board. 'We never even ate curry. And I like a good curry.' He takes a cup of rice from the giant bag he also bought from the shop and cooks himself a good lunch.

He sits in the garden with his meal and stares at the plants, afterwards he pulls a few weeds from the ground and feels pleased that it's rained so much and that the plants seem to be growing by themselves. He's not sure what Mary was doing for all that time in the garden but he thinks that there are more things he could be doing, more things that he doesn't know about, that he wishes he'd learnt as she had. When she mentioned it.

But he didn't take it in, he didn't take an interest, he didn't have the interest. And now that tiny spark of interest was there. He kind of understood, a little. Now he'd got a new, bare garden that he wanted to make nice. He'd started getting a few pots. He wished he'd brought the ones from the old garden. But he'd just left them there, thought it was his time, to start again, make his own choices.

Some things he'd planted had started to grow. First, the plant on the window sill. It had flowered and then flowered again. In the garden at the end of last summer, he'd planted a few pots and now one of them was starting to flower again too. One tiny little red flower had popped out, but he could see more buds, potential bursts of red, coming. 'I'm doing alright he thinks, I'm doing everything, I'm managing, how could I have worried I couldn't cope without her?'

At 2.30 he walks back up to the road again, and stands on the opposite side waiting for his customers. As the first come out of the school he sees them build up into a trail and then a line and then a crowd walking swaying, jangling with bags, carrying coats, the first arriving at speed on scooters, their mums chatting away behind, he smiles at them and gets his arm firm, ready to take his stick out into the road. The school traffic has built up again, as the crowd approaches he holds up his lollipop and his hand to the car ahead, and it slows he walks out into the centre and halts the traffic on other side too. The children begin to cross, swarms of them crossing, some smiling and saying thank you. He hears the siren in the distance, but the children are busy crossing and everything else is going very well.

Above their heads and behind the parked cars he sees the red flashing lights, the red engine, he looks down to the people in front of him and in that moment he makes a choice. He holds his lollipop firm and he stands tall. I know what I'm doing now, he thinks to himself, and watches the line of people who have looked at the fire engine and back at him and continue to cross the road under his watch. He holds onto his stick firm and the last kids are crossing, 'Quick, quick!' The mums and dads say. He looks up to see the fire-fighters approaching, 'You need to move!' They shout. He stands firm. The last kid is crossing, but they are there by his side, they are holding his elbows and lifting him, heels off the ground, back to the roadside.

'Get your hands off me!'

The parents turn but keep on walking, some of the cars nip through the space, the rest are waiting for the fire engine to pass, watching the old man, sniggering, pointing. 'You need to move when we come,' they say, 'this is important, there's a fire.'

They jump back onto the moving fire engine, sirens whirring and he waits, leaning against the wall, his body shaking now, trying to stand upright.

Unlikely deposits

part 1

Suddenly there he was, this stranger, stomping through the house in his big boots. And while she was grateful for the short notice she still couldn't help looking at the muddy marks he was leaving on the carpet for her to clean up afterwards. 'Yes, the storm's coming,' he said.

'Is there a storm coming?'

'You just said there was.'

'Did I? Oh, I said it was windy out. I didn't know about the storm coming.' He looked at her for a moment before turning to study the washing machine.

'Storm Jewel, going to hit us tonight.' He struggled to get down to the floor and she wondered if this would be a quick job.

'Storm Jewel?'

'Yes they've used up the list of names, only use them three times apparently, so they've gone back to a list they used to use in the seventies. Storm Barbara and Storm Jewel! Jewels all lasted three days.'

'Three days?'

'Yep. Named after what's left on the sand when it's whipped the sea into a frenzy.' He glanced across at her woolly knee socks.

Mrs White's manners were urging her to carry on the conversation but her body was fidgeting. 'Do you know how long you'll be? It's just... I need to pick up the children.'

'Can't tell. Depends what the problem is. I'll be okay here if you want to go and get them.'

Got to trust people, she thought.

'Are you related to Ray?' He asked as she left.

'No, not related.'

'Just, you look a bit like someone in his family.'

The car door wouldn't open in the wind. She forgot about the man in the house. As they ran to get back in, their hair swept up around their faces, flicking over their heads, trying to fly away with the leaves. 'We're in the middle of the storm!' Her daughter Alice shouted. 'The eye of Storm Jewel!'

They spotted a toothy gap in the neighbours' fence. The washing machine man was head bent in his van, illuminated by the front light, as though he were in the cockpit of an aeroplane soaring through the night towards them. Hope it's good news, Mrs White thought.

Inside, getting their shoes and coats off, getting the children to go up, getting the lights on, running the bath, she forgot him again. Until there was a knock at the door and there he was, with a tight round belly, collar poking out of his jumper. And big boots. He strutted through the house in his big dirty boots, until he was where he wanted to be, and held up his phone to show her the picture of a hole the size of a ping-pong ball in the rubber lining of her machine.

'So what can you do?' Anything would help. She was over last year's solitary melt downs: the oven door breaking with the dinner still inside; the butternut squash exploding, tattooing her bare arms, painting the entire kitchen a sticky yellow; the corked wine spraying the ceiling red.

But he said, 'Can't do anything about that, love.'

'How much do I owe you then?'

'Are you related to Ray?'

'No.' This time she toyed with saying yes. 'He does my plumbing jobs. Said he couldn't fix the machine though. Gave me your number.'

Then, when she'd paid with his remote wireless gadget, with a discount on account of knowing Ray, he said, 'Don't suppose you want a reconditioned machine?'

'Is it a good make?'

'Well I have a Spanish and a German Bosch. One poor quality, the other very good. Remind me again, are you related to Ray?'

'No. How much for the good one?'

'200… And I can bring it tonight.'

'Are you sure you want to come out again tonight?'

'I can do it if you need it.'

So here they were in the small kitchen again, him huffing and puffing and her hanging around, after the kids were in bed. Pulling the old one out and huffing and puffing down on the floor pushing the new one in. And he says, as she watches, 'If your husband has any work stuff he wants to put in, this'll do the job.'

'My future husband.'

'Well, if your future husband wants to put his overalls in, this'll do it.'

'I'll ask him when I meet him.'

And when it was finally in and she was typing her payment

into the machine again, he was standing quite close and saying, 'I was single too. Did internet dating.'

'Apparently it's the modern way.'

'Trouble with those women,' he said, 'was that they all wanted someone tall, rich and handsome.'

'Oh yes,' she said, trying to be kind, 'and we all know he doesn't exist.'

'I don't really get along with my girlfriend,' he said. 'She's too young. People say I'm really lucky. But...' He was looking Mrs White in the eye.

'Yeah. But it's how you get along. Right?' And she finished the transaction quickly, hoping it was safe, and smiled broadly. 'Thanks so much for coming out tonight.'

Then he was gone and all that was left was the smaller washing machine that didn't fit in the gap, and the black marks all over the floor. Still, least it's done, she'd thought, locking up the house as Storm Jewel raged around them.

The next day Mrs White tried the new washing machine, already suspicious of it, with its out of date labels. The first settings she tried left the washing soaked. Eventually she found one – the longest – that worked.

When it finished the load, fully drained, she pulled open the door and water spat and dribbled from the ring. She checked the lining and found a plaster and two clips. She didn't recognise them. During the next wash – and she had bags of catching up to do, because she'd used up towel after towel to catch the leak – she saw hairs collecting at the front of the machine. Are they our hairs? She thought. By the following morning, Storm Jewel still whooped outside, and a synthetic floral odour crept from under the kitchen door.

Finally the weekend arrived and brought sunshine. One more wash left to do, might as well get it in, she thought that Friday evening after the kids had gone to their dad's. The machine rattled and vibrated and roared as it peaked and Mrs White sat listening with a glass of red wine.

This time when the washing machine spat at her she saw something colourful in the lining. A large green stone that glinted in the dipping sunlight when she put it on the counter. 'I'm sure that's not ours,' she said.

Unlikely deposits

part 2

It was the following Saturday, sitting in Go Bananas indoor playground, when she spotted him at the table in front of her. She probably wouldn't have noticed, but he wore the same tight jumper and a collar, and the same earnest expression he'd worn about the hole in the drum. He was standing over a younger woman, a girl, long straight hair, looking up at him, kids crawling all over her.

Mrs White went back to her list, but over the course of the next few hours she couldn't help thinking something wasn't right. She'd been feeling a little suspicious all week about this so-called refurbed washing machine, peering at its out-of-date labels, with only the longest programme working and then finding all those unidentified objects.

And now the door was stuck with Alice's new nightie inside.

Of course she'd already allowed herself to think that he couldn't have known about the machine; that she was just being paranoid, untrusting. But now she thought a little more negatively.

It could have been the disappointing dishwater coffee she was drinking that made her think differently. But what if he had made that hole when she'd popped out to pick up the kids? What if he charged her for looking at her lovely big washer and then took it away? That photo of a hole that he showed her might not have even been her machine! Then he went off and got her some 'refurbed' one, huffed and puffed in her kitchen at 10 o'clock at night while the kids were asleep, and charged her another 200 quid on top! All done and dusted in one evening. A dribbling old machine harbouring all manner of other people's deposits, and a tired desperate *single* mum needing a washing machine that he'd never see again. Too tired or wouldn't dare call him.

She put down her pen and picked up her phone. She text him a message right there and then and actually saw him pick up his phone, ponder and write something back. *I'm away for two weeks*, he put, *will try to contact you when I get back.* Well Mrs White did not know what to do.

His eyes flicked past hers, not knowing her at all. The young woman was looking up toward the top frame, a screeching child called down. His mouth pursed, the washing machine man turned and strode to the frame entrance. He marched in, was asked to take his boots off by an assistant, scowled, shouted up, had to take his boots off and went in to get that kid from way up above.

Mrs White couldn't really believe her eyes, such a stroke of luck, such an opportunity, that shouldn't, couldn't, be passed up. She didn't really know at that point what she would do with it, but she was making her way through the chairs and piles of discarded jumpers, the odd shoes littering the floor. All she could see were the boots. She grabbed them. They were heavier than she thought. Nearly dropping one, she moved along the edge of the front of the climbing frame, around the outer edge of the room, in case anyone had noticed.

Looking back the scene was unchanged; his girlfriend was pouring over a magazine, the rest of the room in its usual disorder. Kids were running to their jugs of drink, she was walking towards the exit with someone else's boots.

Of course she couldn't actually leave the building because her own kids, unnaturally red-faced, were at their table watching her while slurping down their squash. She shuffled toward them, lowering the boots to her hip trying to make them less obvious.

'What are they?' said Alice.

'Just boots. I bought them at that shop upstairs.'

'Why?'

'Because I thought I could wear them in the garden.'

'They look very big.'

'They are big. Good for gardening. It's time to go,' she said, putting the boots under the table.

'Five minutes!' They were already running off.

She pushed her jumper over the boots by her feet, and sat there as he came out of the tunnel with kid in hand, pulling him towards his mum.

Mrs White saw him turn to go back for the boots, peering around, searching for them, wandering up and down, looking for someone to help him, 'Have you seen my boots?' She can almost hear him from there. She looks back down at her list. He didn't recognise her, wouldn't suspect thing.

Her kids arrived again, grasping at cups, sloshing the squash over the sides. 'Let's go.' Bending and covering the boots like a dog in a blanket, while the kids take forever to get their own shoes on. 'Come on,' she urges. She can see the washing machine man, also red-faced, pacing the area looking up and around, not noticing her even when his gaze flicks past hers.

Finally with everything in her arms, she's pushing at the locked exit gate, waiting for the attendant to notice them, to unlock it, until she's falling through it, until they're outside the main doors. The rain is still heavy, the kids are jumping over puddles as she rushes towards the park, hugging the boots like an injured puppy. When they cross the bridge over the swollen river, Alice shouts: 'Look at the river – let's do pooh sticks!'

'Great idea,' Mrs White says, unwrapping her load.

Unlikely deposits

part 3

It was the week we knew Tyson had to die. I took him for his slow walk on Sunday morning and he still snuffled up the bits of pizza and lumps of vomit left outside the shops on Station Road. That's when I had the idea that I'd order him a Domino's for his last meal. I was going to make it special.

'Really?' Claire said. 'Just for the dog? A whole pizza?'

'Yep. It's his last supper so we're gonna give him his favourite meal. Right, Jorden?'

'Can I get one too?'

'Yep.'

'All to myself?'

'Yep.'

Anyway that's what I did. The dog was beside himself on Tuesday night when the delivery guy arrived and I put a whole large box on the floor for him. You should have seen his little face. 'Waste of money,' she said.

We took him in on Wednesday and said our goodbyes before

he had the injection and snoozed for the last time. I was choked, I have to say. The vet said they'd take him away but I wasn't having any of it. I saw the little guy into the world and we were going to see him out of it. Give him a proper wake, invite the family over to say their goodbyes too. Have a gathering. With snacks and drinks.

She wasn't so keen on the idea, but she'd never liked him much. He wasn't hers really, he was mine. Always had been, by my side in the last marriage too. That dog lasted longer than my marriages! He'd have lasted much longer too, the vet had said, if the cancer hadn't got him.

It was just before he was about to have his injection that the phone buzzed. Afterwards I checked the message and saw it was about a machine.

Can you help me? I'm sure you didn't realise but the washing machine you sold me is dribbling water from the ring and now the door's locked shut. Please could you come and look at it.

I swiped it away and forgot about it. The phone buzzed again while I was in the car with the dog across the kids laps and buzzed again after we laid him out on the dining room table. 'Put this cloth down then,' Claire had said, and sure it looked good with the dog in the middle of the cloth, like a proper wake, where everyone comes and pays their last respects.

Ray and Helen came from next door and made all the right noises, while we had a beer and I told the story about when I first got him with Angie, and Claire just bashed about in the kitchen. My phone buzzed in my pocket, it was that stupid cow about the machine again. Not good timing with Ray being there either, bet he doesn't get constant messages from crazy women.

I'm sure you won't answer but the machine is faulty, the door's stuck its full of water and my daughter's new nightie is in there.

Like I'd give a toss about her daughter's new nightie at a time like this!

The girls got together in the kitchen and I could hear them giggling. But me and Ray made a plan to bury him Saturday evening, have a little ceremony, stick a cross in the ground and all that. And the good ol' boy said he'd help me dig a grave Saturday morning, under the tree in the garden.

So the dog stayed there for the next two days, we covered him over with a blanket and took it off in the evening. On Friday Phil came over and brought his new girlfriend. He told the kids that he didn't want to move in with her and her kids, because it was too much like hard work. We had a right laugh about that and I was thinking he's onto something there.

That night I woke up to the first rumbles of storm Barbara and as the rain spilled from the sky I kept thinking about digging the hole for the dog.

Ray made an excuse, said his mother-in-law was sick, so I got myself out there and was digging in the wet. Which was frankly better than being in the house with that grumpy cow and the kids climbing the walls. At lunch-time she made lasagne and I decided to sort it out, said I'd take them to Go Bananas, for a treat, even though they'd done nothing all morning and I'd been the one digging the hole for Tyson. I said to her, the kids could run off and she could read her mag. So we got there and everyone else in the town had the same bloody idea.

I got another text from this woman about the machine, thought I might as well answer her:

Sorry about your machine but I'm away for the next two weeks. Could come and see it when I get back.

She replies to that almost instantly. In capitals.

I CAN'T GET THE DOOR OPEN. I CAN'T GET THE NIGHTIE OUT OF THE MACHINE. I NEED HELP.

The kids kept coming over and clinging onto Claire and fighting and telling, so I carried on fiddling with that new website for the shop. I think we'd all had enough, Claire was seething at me to go and sort Jorden out – he was calling down from the very top of the climbing frame. And wouldn't come down even when I shouted him to. So I tried to get in there to get him, and one of the young attendants told me I needed to take my boots off! For God's sake. I never take my boots off! Not even at home!

When it was sorted out, I dragged him down by his ear. I couldn't find my boots. The place was sprawling with kids and shoes, we couldn't find my boots anywhere. I had to send the others home while I carried on looking with the stupid girl that had made me take them off. They were nowhere to be seen, even after the last kids had gone.

In the end they gave me two Go Bananas bags to put over my feet and I had to get back through the pouring rain like that. Got in and put them up in front of the fire, tingling all over with pins and needles and shivering and then boiling up.

That night Claire shook my arm. 'There's a bad smell!' she said. 'Coming from downstairs,' she said. 'Go and look!'

I felt the thick air prickle my arms as my legs wobbled down the stairs. The stench was stronger as I got further down, thought we'd had some kind of weird burglary or something.

But the dining room was covered in shit and sick and insides and the mess was on the floor and in the walls; globules of blood and sick and shit all over the dining room table and Tyson looking like an deflated puppet dribbling pink potato chunks.

'Shit and Jesus!' I said. 'Get down here! It's the dog! You're gonna have to clear up this mess, Claire!'

'I ain't clearing up one more thing after that dog, or you!' she said. I heard her pulling things about in the bedroom. She dragged down the big case she came with and said 'I'll call the kids in the morning.'

'Where are you going?'

'Don't ask me. I ain't telling you. The wipes are under the sink.'

The little green lamp

The orange curtains are drawn carefully together in the evening. They are drawn together slowly, and every morning they are pulled apart. In between, in the day time, they gradually fade in the hot sun. On their backs are the stripes where the light has clawed but could not spread.

'It's alright for you,' says the left curtain. 'You are shaded by the fence. The sun doesn't sit fully on you every day, burning into you, tattooing you with its pale yet lethal light, sucking the orange from you in strips so you look like the deck chairs they used to get out in the summer.'

'Stop complaining,' says the right hand curtain. 'The sun doesn't sit fully on my back, no, only partially. But the shade from the fence makes me miserable and the light from the sun cheers me up. I wish I had more sun. How can you complain about the sun on your back?'

'If you had it on the whole of your back then you would know. As it is, you believe that it would make you happy, because you have forgotten what it is like to have the sun on your back all day long.'

'You're wrong. I remember when we were at the other house,

in the little boy's bedroom. The sun sat on both our backs in the morning and was gone by the afternoon. I was happy in the mornings.'

'That was a long time ago.'

'Yes, but I remember it well. Each day the little boy got up and pulled us apart with his plump hands and stared into the garden from his bedroom window and whooped with delight at the toys they'd put out for him. He looked at the new day, his blue car, his paddling pool. I felt his soft hands and his excitement. A happy time.'

'I remember it too,' said the striped curtain.

'And now we're here at this long window in this small house, able to see everything that goes on all day long, and the little boy and the little girl, now big, run between us without even noticing us.'

'Well, I for one do not remember the old house,' booms the fat paper lantern. 'Do you?' He shouts at his twin at the other end of the room.

'Are you talking to me? If you are, stop shouting. I'm only here.'

'I said, do you remember the old house?'

'Not I,' says the other lampshade. 'I'm new. So are you. I'm happy here. In this house, at this end of the room. I see everything that is going on, and I watch what the woman is doing when the kids have gone to bed. She sits still on this sofa near me.'

'Yes, but she never turns you on, does she?' laughs the left curtain.

'Not yet, no. But I know she will. I look good at this end of the room. Look at me, I mean there's a reason she chose us. Look at my fine wooden frame, the delicate white paper stretched between the bamboo canes. One day, when she has a guest, she will turn me on and show me off. For now, she just uses the small lamp in the corner with the ridiculous green shade, that doesn't suit it at all. Such a small dim light and a silly green shade. She's saving me for best, I know it.'

'What do you think's happening to us?' Says the left hand curtain, which is now folded beneath the other.

'We're just going somewhere else,' says the right hand curtain.

'Oh my god,' says the left. 'Where now? What next? I've seen those landfill sights on the television, we'll end up in one of those, I know it! With flies our only living companions! No children, no lady, just flies.'

'Try not to worry,' says the right curtain, wishing that the lady hadn't started turning on the television. The left curtain feels the right curtain quiver. He begins to weep.

'Why did I complain about the sun on my back? When our life, our end will be so much worse?'

The other sticks of furniture are silent, respecting the difficulties the orange curtains now face. The white lantern is quiet above them. He is sorry because he has become used to the two curtains, moaning and chattering and opening and closing. He feels lucky that he continues to be white, that the woman has started to dust him, and that the other lantern has recently been lit. She is the most beautiful object he has ever seen. He feels guilty for thinking such thoughts now while the orange curtains suffer. But then, they *are* old, he thinks. They came from the old house, they are faded, they do not look like they fit in here with us now. When they are replaced it will be surprising the difference that will come about. He wonders who the new curtains will be and starts daydreaming about them. I wonder what colour they will be. Teal? Which fabric? Velvet?

'Helloo over there!' The other white lantern cries. 'Helloooo!' She has become more verbal, spritelier since the lady started turning her on. 'How are things?'

'As you'd expect,' says the fat lantern in as soft a voice as he can muster.

'Oh deary me,' she says, 'a dreadful affair, losing someone like this.'

'They've not gone yet,' says the little green lamp softly.

'Who asked you?' says the white lantern. 'Such a dreadful affair.'

The left curtain is still weeping when the lady comes into the room, turning on the first lantern and then the second, and picking up the pile.

'Goodbye,' they whisper, 'goodbye all.'

The lady carries them upstairs. The left curtain cannot see or think for weeping. She takes them into the bathroom where she places them on the toilet seat.

She picks up the right curtain, holds it up in a half fold, peering underneath, looking at its back. Then she drops it to the floor and picks up the left curtain, again looking it up and down on both sides. She drops it into a cold bath.

They spend the evening together in the bathroom, and when she has finished with them, she leaves them hanging on a clothes horse to dry.

When she's gone the left curtain says, 'Can you see me? Can you see what's happened?'

'No not quite,' says the right hand curtain.

'I am orange! I am not striped, I am orange again!'

The right curtain lets out a big, stomach gurgling laugh, slips off the airer and slides down the side of the bath.

Acknowledgements

Thank you to Patricia and the growing Patrician Press gang.

Thank you to Colchester WriteNighters, a warm and supportive writing community, all writing their own masterpieces. Many of these stories began their short lives at WriteNight.

Thanks to Sue Dawes, Sarah Armstrong and Adrian May, the fastest bestest editors/proofers/writer friends in town.

Thank you readers Polly and Jo, for reading and great comments.

Thanks to my family and friends, for sustaining my existence, plus the story ideas.

Thank you to my work colleagues who continue to work hard, sometimes in difficult circumstances, but always having a laugh, and sometimes a cry, over biscuits at break.

Other collections by Emma Kittle-Pey

Fat Maggie and other stories by Emma Kittle-Pey was first published in 2013 and reprinted in 2017.

Paperback edition 978-0-9927235-3-8

E-book edition 978-0-9575751-6-5

This quirky and subtly witty collection tackles daily interactions at home, in the workplace, on holiday or at social events. The Fat Maggie animal-related tales were written with traditional tales and morals in mind, contributing to the dead-pan humour they evoke.